THE GIRL WITH SPIDERS IN HER HAIR

Hailey Slade

First Published in Great Britain in 2023 by
Drawn to a Story

ISBN: 978-1-7384222-0-3
Designed by Cath Brew, www.drawntoastory.com

Illustrations by Hailey Slade

This book is for my inner child

Acknowledgements

To Cath, for holding my hand through this process (literally). From taking me on journeys to find my inner child, nurturing us both, to the creation in its physical form. The story would have remained hidden without your guidance, for which I'm eternally grateful.

To my family for always being so understanding, supportive and communicative. You helped teach me to empathise and relate.

My witchy coven and soul sisters, who always have my back and give me the much-needed fire in my gut to stay the course.

Jengo and Shiva, for always welcoming me on my journeys.

Prologue

Upon completion, these words stayed hidden in my grasp for over a year. I wanted to share them so I didn't feel so lost, but the anxiety of how my thoughts and feelings may be perceived made me cling onto them tighter.

I pondered over removing darker, truthful sentiments, so that the story may read kinder for others, but then I realised, once again, that was me trying to 'fit in'. It was me moulding my life and experiences around the neurotypical world, protecting other people's feelings, rather than my own, and leaving them like loose change at the bottom, below everyone else who fits into this world. If my tale helps one person, then my mission has succeeded.

This is honesty.

My story is dark because it is my hidden reality. It reveals experiences as an autistic person and how I've spent my life and energy masking and mimicking discomfort of others. Without the harshness of my reality, nothing will change. I no longer feel the need, or want, to fit in. Freedom comes from sharing our truth.

If you have a family member who is neurodiverse, this book will inform and educate you about how to develop empathy, and support your loved ones in ways you may not have once understood.

For those of you reading, with autism, it's my ambition to make you feel validated and less alone. Remember, even if you prefer it that way physically, you are not alone.

Once upon a time, in a small, picturesque town, there lay a young girl at the top of a steep hill. A mess of wild auburn hair that caught the sun like a dancing flame, eyes as dark as the bottom of a well and robes sullied with mud and rips from her eager adventures. She lay on her back in the grass under the sun of a late summer afternoon. Her gaze followed a path downhill that was lined with trees and framed a small medieval town in the distance - the haze of heat rising from the warm ground creating a liquid feel to the air that shimmered with the feel of magic.

Rolling onto her front, she scratched her head as spiders fell from her hair. Watching them intently as they crawled down her hand, she smiled feeling their soft steps tickling - such mysteriously misunderstood creatures feared by many, but she was captivated.

Looking around where she lay, she admired the barbed shapes formed by the brambles and thorns that safely encompassed her. The delicate scent of coconut drifted from the Gorse bush with its paradoxical flowers.

Here, she was safe, she was protected. Spiky dominating shrubs created a barricade from the outside world. No one would bother her here. That was, until the sun began to creep towards the horizon, turning her favourite orange tones, reality threatening to steal the peace she found within, albeit fleetingly. A recurring feeling of dread set in around this time of day, as she awaited the call beckoning her to return home.

This disturbance came from her older sister who belonged to the hierarchical group of teenagers that ran the social networks of the town. This collective was a terrifying sight for the girl with spiders in her hair.

"Come on, it's time to go!"

The voices grew louder. Footsteps drew closer, the crack of branches, the kick of stones, as one landed beside her, scattering dust which settled sharply in her eyes - a rude awakening from the sheer bliss she was in moments ago.

But laying there felt so right! So safe, so warm, so comforting, despite the scrapes that stung and bled, despite the grazes that wept from her clumsy hurdle into her special hidden place, and also despite the dizzying feeling that the world turned beneath her.

It was a comfort, like the rocking of a babe, a sensory reset, the heavy weight of gravity magnetising her to the ground, like a fly caught in a spider's web, and cradled by the earth's gentle movements. She once spoke to the elder folk about this sensation, that was, until they mocked her, laughing dismissively.

She vowed to keep these thoughts and feelings buried deep, for not many understood her. The self-preservation settled around her like a warm blanket.

"We have to get home for dinner, now!" came her sister's voice, the only one she cared about pleasing. Looking up with a longing, an urgency to be seen by her, with an envy so strong, she was all of the things our girl wasn't. She was all of the traits that allowed a person to blend in, that stopped people noticing someone in all of the unkind ways they noticed her.

"Weirdo, freak, ginger, tubby, goofy, clumsy, mucky pup, ugly duckling," you name it, she'd heard it. Some were meant as endearments, others as 'jokes', but none of them felt nice.

Her sister, the apple of her eye, everything she wanted to be, pretty, popular and slim, she 'fit' into that world at the bottom of the tree-lined path - not like our girl, a square peg in a round hole.

"Time to go home" gazing up, trying and hoping to catch her sister's eye, but too soon her sister turns away so the others don't notice their transaction. Is she embarrassed, even ashamed of her little sister? In their short transactions, her sister's dismissals feel so personal to the girl with spiders in her hair.

It's not until many years later that our girl would know or even understand that darkness, and her sister's own battles.

To her, she went about her life in the only way she knew, the way that felt right. She didn't know why others found this such a hardship, or even how her life impacted their day so much. Observing and mimicking the interactions of the others in the village so she may fit in, clearly wasn't working.

Our girl knew she needed to try harder, to do better to hide herself from the evils that lurked in this uncomfortable world. The reality hit like a cannonball.

This meant more time spent amongst the folk and less time escaping the harsh reality, less time telling tales to her empathic creatures on the hill, the only friends that truly understood her. That was all except for her trusty stead and companion, Odin.

Odin was a protective force, a lump of

muscle in the form of a giant black dog, her pillar of strength, her confidant. They were connected, laying together for hours upon her bedroom floor, as she sang with her head upon his stomach, feeling serene, safe, whole, him snoring and twitching contentedly.

Fear filled her every day that she had to rise and ready herself to embark on the dark treacherous path to the town, down steep rocky outcrops, through haunted pathways where shadows danced behind her, taunting and tickling her hair in the wind. They pulled at the torn threads of her bookpack, until she ran crying, frantically looking for help, but there was no safety, not until the time came to return home, to her sanctuary, to Odin, or to her blessed hill top.

The horrifying path lead her alone and flustered to the bustling town centre where all manner of folk made life look so easy and fun. They smiled during their excited social exchanges, reaching out to help those they knew well, the sort of help she'd never be offered. She was the goblet with the crack that leaks the sacred holy waters, an inconvenience for all.

The crowd bristled by, purposefully barging limbs to unsteady her pace, laughing as she trips. And then a heavy blow comes, blindsiding her, knocking her hard against the towering fortress walls. Sliding down to the wet muddy ground, she bites her lip hard purposefully, a distraction from the searing pain in her skull, forcing herself not to cry. Don't give in! Don't let them see! Don't give them what they want! Their laughter will only grow louder, their pointing fingers sharper.

Time stops. The marketplace freezes, stars in her vision, a static feeling of magic in the air, hairs standing on end. A warm soft hand clasps hers. Hot shivers surge up her arms and through her body, an overwhelmingly confusing feeling. This utter bafflement causes her to shake her head and she focuses in on the large kind hand around her small dirty one.

She's aided to her feet, lifted with ease and steadied. She notices the ripped satchel carrying her books laying in a puddle of filth. Straightening her wet and tatty robe, and finally looking up, she meets the shimmering eyes of the Prince.

The expanse of a moment that's so fleeting yet feels it lasts a lifetime, shocks, not only the girl with spiders in her hair, but the whole marketplace.

Silent, the crowd step back aghast, all eyes darting from the handsome Prince to the dirty village girl. His blazing blue eyes transfixed on her lost shameful face. "Are you alright?" Waiting for a response, his caring eyes searching hers. She feels his genuine concern. This must be a dream, or at least a spell?! Summoning the courage, she forces an answer from her lips, a false confirmation she'd heard others relay in these moments. She doesn't have an answer, a script she can call upon when her mind is blank and the mask is slipping.

Squirming under the gaze of the entire marketplace, she nods solemnly. Why won't they just turn away?! The facade is crumbling, the tears are hot like lava bubbling up in her eyes. She thanks him graciously with a low clumsy curtsy as she grabs her sodden book bag from the slop, gathers up her skirt and runs! She runs to find safety, runs to find peace from the now hysterically laughing crowd. She just wants to dissolve in darkness, but she knows of no place she can fully let go.

Stumbling again, the laughter erupting behind her is like a wave crashing on the shore. Exhaustion beckoning, her legs give way, tumbling to the ground. She finds herself in a dark, wonky alley between various magical shops and apothecaries in a part of town those laughing would never frequent. Oh no, they'd not be seen here amongst the outcasts, the 'lower' class, the fae, the warlocks, the magical folk, the have nots.

Sobbing heavily, fighting for air, she presses her eye lids until she sees stars. She feels nothing else, only her cold wet muddy fingers, a painful necessary distraction, as she tries her hardest to bring herself into the present.

A loud bang from nearby startles her. Jumping, she meets the gaze of huge pair of eyes at her feet. A small scaley bright orange goblin blinks up at her, extending a claw onto her leg, as if in a warm gesture of comfort.

She catches her breath, resting her chin on her knees, whilst hugging them tightly to her chest and bracing her pounding heart which is knocking loudly on her rib cage. She smiles down at the kind creature, hooking a finger into its claw. It tilts its head and makes a small questioning sound.

These beings speak her language. The town folk aren't able to hear it, but here among the 'outcasts' all creatures and beings alike have a way of communicating with each other. Not by words, like the small-minded towns people, but by a sense, a feeling, a gut instinct, intuition.

The goblin crawls up her legs curling into a ball on her knees. Leaning towards one another, they touch their foreheads and close their eyes, when the brightest flash of golden light fills her vision. The ground falls away and she's transported.

⚹   ⚹   ⚹

Standing looking down at her bare feet in the mud - a familiar sight, in an unfamiliar place - an enchanted woodland, with colourful plants she's never seen before of all shapes and sizes. There's vibrancy she never knew existed. Flowers pulsate, the air busy with pixies and small creatures going about their business, accompanied by a high-pitched hum of their flighty wings darting around with intent. Colourful orbs catch the rays of sun penetrating through the thick canopy above.

Something ahead of her sparkles, catching her eye as she's drawn to an uphill path leading to a doorway made from trees. A bright shimmering light seeps in from around its edges as a captivatingly beautiful red-haired goddess greets her.

She's beaming, pleased to see the girl with spiders in her hair, as if she knows and has been waiting, just for her. In awe, she searches her mind for words that do not come. Speechless, freezing on the spot, our girl is engulfed by her presence, her grace, kindness and love. Who is this lady?

As she's pulled into a firm embrace, so comforting, the tears well in our girl's eyes. She feels safe in a lifetime of chaos. Slowly she looks up, meeting a kind gaze. With a powerful yearning, wanting to be her, *one day*, she thinks, *I'll grow into a woman like her, that's something I can hope for!*

The beautiful red head takes a hold of her shoulders. Stepping back, she searches her face. "Don't let go!" she wants to cry, but again words fail her. Then it happens. She feels herself falling, falling backwards, through the ground. The earth is moving again.

Engulfed by a blackness, so dark she cannot see her own hand in front of her face, the overwhelming sense of fear rises. She hears the crack of branches around her as if there's something or someone moving towards her, looming.

A pale cold light from a waning crescent moon illuminates the silvery wet ground. The twisted outline of old haunted trees arch and flex in the roaring wind, creating shadows that stretch and creep across the uneven woodland floor towards her. The hairs on the back of her neck stand on end.

Feeling a dominating presence approaching her, she hears a rasping catching breath - the monsters in the dark. The stench and feel of hot breath in her ear send sharp shivers down her spine, teeth gnashing at her face and neck, a repulsive sensation as she tries to wriggle free - but not before she's backed against a rough tree trunk covered in damp cold moss and hideous bugs that crawl all over her.

Tall thin long-limbed creatures grab and paw at her, with their gnarled clawed fingers, pulling at her body

not listening to her pleas to stop. Clutching at knives, dismissing her words, pointing and winding their creepy long fingers all over her, they clutch themselves, pinning her down as she tries to scramble away on the wet ground.

Branches pull and catch her ragged clothing as she tries to run from the monsters that follow so closely like a shadow. A harsh flash of lightening momentarily highlights the vascular sinewy extremities that stretch towards her, reaching. An ear-splitting loud clap of thunder penetrates the black as her name pulsates like a drum in every tone and pitch within her mind.

There is no escaping the overwhelm of every sense, every feeling, inside and out. She wants it all to stop! Collapsing against a knotty hollowed out tree stump, she begs to be taken to her barricade on the hilltop, to her sanctuary, to Odin!

Suddenly, a hue of calming orange light glows warmly, softly breaking through the blackness, beckoning her to a friendly place. It allows just enough clarity through the darkness for her to turn and run, anywhere has to be better than here!

The light from around the magical doorway opens up to reveal the beautiful lady, her hands extended and she's calling to our girl, beckoning her to safety. With eyes clenched shut, she runs towards the doorway, outstretched arms, tears streaming, until the gentle embrace encompasses her once again. Feeling the crash of

emotions, and unable to grip the edges of the mask any longer, she gives in. The damn breaks. She sobs and wails. She's safe. She knows it.

Feeling comforting hands stroke her back and soothe her, encouraging words of kindness and empathy whispered in her ear, she knows it's ok.

In this moment, she can let the barriers down. All those years of struggling under their weight, holding them up with all of her might, she no longer has the energy. Eventually, catching her breath, she can't help but ask this kind beauty, "Who are you?!"

"Why dear love, I'm you! There is a light at the end of this dark tunnel, and that light is you."

Waking with a start, a full body jolt, the familiar scent of coconut fills her senses. She opens her eyes to see the trees above in that well-known friendly arch, the thorns and brambles engulfing her, an ordinary safety, sitting up, recognising her comforting hilltop.

Squinting through her blurry sleep-heavy eyes to gain clarity on the far away town at the bottom of the tree lined path, she feels the familiar tickle of spiders in her hair as one lowers itself on a delicate string of web in front of her eyes so close, she cannot focus.

She feels her eyelashes flex under its weight, a gift, so precious to her, something so small. Even though others would run screaming, she feels blessed. In that moment, laying back on the comfort of the warm ground, in the mid-afternoon sun, she's content, knowing that this phase won't last. These feelings won't last.

She will be her own light. She is filled with hope for her future. Deep in thought, *I will not 'fit in'. And that's the point. That's ok, and that's where I find my own world, my own peace, my own happiness within.*

The End

About the Author

Hailey enjoys spending her time hiking the south west coast path with her little dog Rocco, cooking wholesome vegan and gluten free food, practicing yoga, getting lost in reading fantasy tales and dabbling in practical witchcraft with her coven. Being out in nature is where she finds most of her creativity and inspiration. A Dorset gal, born and bred, she still resides in her beautifully scenic hometown.

By day she is a Tattoo Artist who enjoys decorating people's skin with colourful, fun images inspired by her love for Halloween, Tim Burton, Disney and Harry Potter. Giving people unique tributes on their skin is a pleasure and a space she is very grateful to hold.

She began writing fairy tales as a young child, sitting amongst the trees, but many of them were hidden away and lost to time.

After her late diagnosis of Autism Spectrum Disorder (Asperger's Syndrome), she felt more confident to share her perspective of growing up in a world that didn't 'fit'.

Check out her tattoos on Instagram @tattoosbyhai.com